The COCONÖT Book

A Story about Faith and Cancer Survival

Written and Illustrated by:
Donn Angel Pérez López

AuthorHouse™
1663 Liberty Drive
Bloomington, IN 47403
www.authorhouse.com
Phone: 1-800-839-8640

Published by AuthorHouse 06/18/2013

ISBN: 978-1-4817-5953-3 (sc)
ISBN: 978-1-4817-5954-0 (e)

Library of Congress Control Number: 2013910168

Any people depicted in stock imagery provided by Thinkstock are models,
and such images are being used for illustrative purposes only.
Certain stock imagery © Thinkstock.

This book is printed on acid-free paper.

authorHOUSE®

Hi there! My name is CoconÖt but my friends call me NÖt.

Since I speak broken English, I like NÖt a lot.

Here I am feeling great because I'm still here with friends and with you.

Looking forward to sharing my story, some tears and new points of view.

I will tell you what happened one warm summer day.

At the time it all seemed quite scary, but it was a blessing I'll now say.

Because I care and because I dare, I will say it over and over again.

As hard as it was then, I find myself here now and with so much to gain.

Let me start my story by sketching an island scene for you.

I love drawing very much and it is my favorite thing to do.

With my pencils I want to get all of the colors just right you see,

especially orange, green and blue because they are friendly like me.

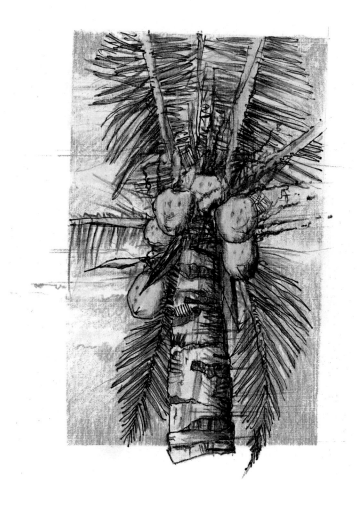

It's nice to remember how the good old times felt to me,

and I can tell you that because deep in my soul there is still more to see.

I am grateful to have an angel of life who gives me love and care.

I know this because I was once in some trouble, as you will become aware.

Everything seems simple when you are feeling happy, alive and well,

when you are facing the waves of life and letting them carry you on their swell.

I found myself drifting along in the motion of life in a nice place I knew,

when suddenly I was confused and did not understand what I was going through..

Something was different and many things were occurring,

all of a sudden I was taking pills, feeling pain and it was time for enduring.

Things were changing so fast, from my body to my spirit,

And I remember shouting, "**I WANT TO LIVE!**" so that everyone could hear it.

Then out of the blue I realized that fewer days appeared funny.

In the place where I found myself only some days were bright and sunny.

The doctors told me that I had cancer and that they didn't know too much.

I had to wait with patience and I felt so out of touch.

I remember when I received the news - the ground trembled and shook.

There comes a time in life when you have no choice but to stop and take a deep look.

Thankfully I had others around me who cared, so I was not on my own.

They were such a great support group and with them I never felt alone.

I call the day I found out "the day of truth" - a moment when I would choose.

As you know in life we have options and in that moment I chose not to lose.

Not to fall or surrender, not to give up or retreat, but to conquer a frightful disease,

because I assure you my friend, cancer was not for me and it gave me no peace.

One day when my doctor checked on me and he asked, "How are you feeling NÖt?"

I responded, "I think I will live Doc! I can take a lot, so give me all you got!

Poke me, treat me, heal me ... and please, say and do what you think you must do and say.

Do what is right and leave the rest to me for God is here with me and forever to stay."

Radiation, chemo, tests and pills – cancer is such a tough deal.

Oh well, just give me some games to play and then I'll tell you how I feel.

As I floated in a sea of patience, I did my best to stay still.

I took in the rays all around me and did it because of my will.

I stayed there and prayed, and though I felt hungry I ate just a little.

I promised to try to eat more later, with a spoon for sure but not through a needle.

WHAT - more Chemo?!

Some things were easier to bear than others, but some were tougher on the quest,

tiredness, queasiness, sadness and sleeplessness – I sure needed some rest!

Suddenly I had no hair and I thought I looked rather funny - what a deal...

I wanted to feel better for a bit and knew that I would when I kneeled.

I felt kind of down that day and just did not want to feel ill,

so I opened my eyes to the sky, said a prayer and then took my "get-better" pill.

"Have patience NÖt", said the Wind while passing close by my side.

"There's still so much to be done - stay strong and keep your spirit open wide.

When you think you're finished and you're feeling selfish,

remember there are still many things to accomplish."

Then the Wind said with more intensity, **"Get ready because you will succeed!**

Just believe it NÖt - you will indeed."

I looked outside and something amazing was happening and I could feel it on my face!

It was the sun - bright, brilliant and yellow and it was filling my empty space.

Energy was something I needed to have a lot of to stay on the healing track,

like now I need a break to soak it in so I'll be right back...

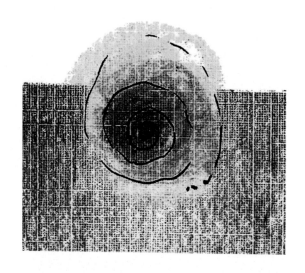

While NÖt is taking a break, you are invited to draw nature around you in these spaces,

And fill the coming pages with lines, circles and colored traces.

Sketch your thoughts in these spaces with coolness and might,

And with pencils imagine a beautiful sunset and a starry night.

Draw circles, dots and many lines.

Open your mind and seek your style.

Try to draw coconuts and sea animals of all kinds,

and jot down some good phrases even if they don't rhyme.

Do not become anxious about anything at all.

Drawing images is like knowing that you have a soul.

It takes practice, time and a spirit of inspiration.

The point is to find your center of gravity and some relaxation.

Practice by making circular motions, squiggles and fast lines.

Relax your hand, focus your eyes and use your mind.

Let it flow and use your imagination and you may even create some healing art.

Here are some samples so you have a good start.

No matter what you do,

don't forget you can use colors like orange and blue.

Our Spanish speaking friend NÖt is back now, it's funny,

he always shows up on warm days and especially when its sunny.

Hi, I'm back and I brought friends and bright sunshine to warm up my core.

Do you want some? Would you accept it? Sharing and giving, I must do more.

Loved ones wanted to care for me then but sometimes they just let me be.

I wondered when I would be done with it all, to float again in the peace of God's sea?

You know, to me cancer was just a word that began with the letter 'c'.

My Spanish speaking friend said, "To life you should always say 'Claro que si'."

Try this amigo: uno, dos, tres . When you don't feel well, just count to tres.

Don't listen to words like 'Sadness' or 'Stress'.

Here are two better words and you can say them with zest -

'Strength' and 'Success'.

Nighttime would come, as it always does, and I wanted it to go by in a flash.

I hoped the nights had a full moon and stars as I waited for the darkness to pass.

It was during nighttime that thoughts seemed to worsen and sadness sometimes snuck in,

but eventually I didn't feel alone anymore and I knew the battle I was going to win.

At the moment of twilight, stars and moon became one as fear battled might.

That's when I found the calm in my heart to have faith and to make it through the night.

And even when things continued to seem unclear and just not right,

I still found peace and with my God I continued to pray and fight.

I looked up and saw that the sky was just a blanket over me

and just above it, I thought, the light was still there ready to let me be.

Through tiny openings in the canvas of an infinite universe, indeed,

I could almost see beyond and with the conviction that I would succeed.

So I needed just a little bit longer to rest,

as I tried to silence my apprehension.

I was together with God at His best,

hopeful that I would start each new day with good direction.

In time, the nights got better and while my eyes were often tired, my spirit was awake.

Sunrises are like moments of celebration and opportunities for more drawings to make.

There is hope in every awakening, a renewed spirit with every dawn.

New life! New joy! "Hang on everyone", I said, as I was ready to be done.

You see, I was tired in the early days and many days during too, but not one day.

The light of that day was out and I was ready to talk and play.

It's so wonderful to see the beginning of a sunrise,

so awesome, so beautiful, so blessed... it was no surprise.

"You know, Doctor," I said, "I am ready to be done and to aim for my best.

Sometimes chemo is too much and quite often I wonder what's next."

Then the Doctor said, "Scars are healing NÖt and you are almost there.

Enjoy life as it comes, together with your loved ones and without despair."

So here you have me God, still surrounding me with friends and places to be.

Time has passed and still with great company, Mother Nature and an everlasting sea.

I will share, oh God, I promise that. Everyday I'll find myself resilient in all.

Determined, faithful and strong, I know that to hopelessness I will not fall.

I'm still here with you and for those who are not - they will always live in my heart.

And with my dear one here by my side, I know we will never be apart.

Face each moment in gratitude and help others find wellness and pleasure.

Understand that life is a treasure and what comes after cannot be measured.

So, adios for now, but remember me and we will stay together in mind and spirit.

I would like to go and see my loved ones and shout, **"I am cured!"** Did you hear it?

I will always try to be at my best, to do what is good and to search for God's light,

because with Him I know that I am free and He will always let it be right.

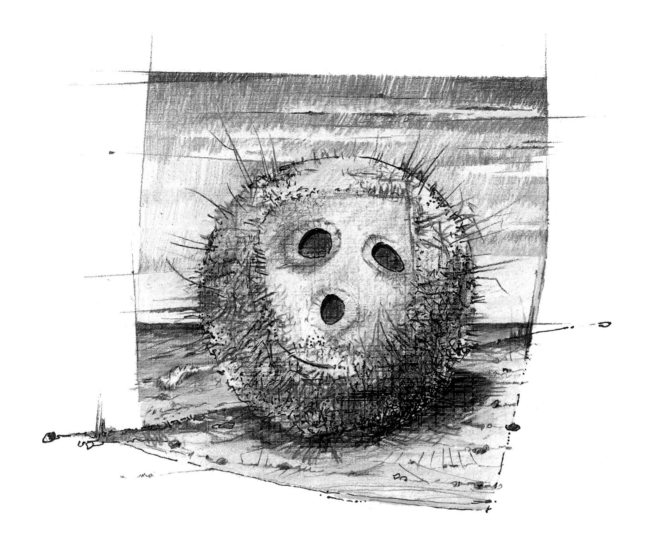

So remember my friend that my name is NÖt and I love God a lot.

Help from my loved ones, along with medicine, hope and faith got me here again.

I believe that there is a mission to complete, because I am still alive and I am NÖt.

I have been blessed and hope you know I will try my best to never, ever complain.

So here from this place I tell you good bye, but just for a little while.

I say that with faith, hope and love, and I will let God reconcile.

My dream is that we would see each other many more times and never be apart,

so that you and I together may draw and create great and beautiful art.

Printed in the United States
by Baker & Taylor Publisher Services